CATCHING WAVES

The #1
Sports Series
for Kids

CATCHING WAVES

Text by Stephanie Peters

LITTLE, BROWN AND COMPANY

New York ⌁ Boston ⌁ London

Little, Brown and Company

Time Warner Book Group
1271 Avenue of the Americas, New York, NY 10020
Visit our Web site at www.lb-kids.com

www.mattchristopher.com

First Edition: June 2006

Matt Christopher® is a registered trademark of
Matt Christopher Royalties, Inc.

Text by Stephanie Peters

Library of Congress Cataloging-in-Publication Data

Peters, Stephanie True, 1965–
    Catching Waves / [text written by Stephanie Peters].— 1st ed.
        p.   cm.
    Summary: Fourteen-year-old Kai Ford, a good surfer who
respects the power of the sea, unfortunately does not always
have the same respect for the privacy of other people.
    ISBN-13: 978-0-316-05848-3 (trade pbk. : alk. paper)
    ISBN-10: 0-316-05848-3 (trade pbk. : alk. paper)
    [1. Surfing — Fiction.   2. Privacy, Right of — Fiction.
3. California — Fiction.]   I. Title.
PZ7.P441833Cat 2006
[Fic] — dc22   2005029482

GV865.R6S86   2005
796.357'092 — dc22   2004020153

10 9 8 7 6 5 4 3 2 1

COM-MO

Printed in the United States of America

CATCHING WAVES

Kai Ford stuck his surfboard into the sand, ran full speed into the ocean, and dove into a wave. The sound of rushing water filled his ears. He broke the surface, tasting salt, and whipped his blond hair out of his eyes with a toss of his head. Then he scanned the ocean horizon. What he saw made him grin. Good-sized waves were rolling in one after another, like lines of soldiers marching toward shore.

Time to rock and roll! He splashed out of the water and crossed the hot sand to his surfboard.

The board was a beauty. At seven feet long, it was known as a shortboard — the best length for doing tight maneuvers on a wave. It was made of fiberglass, foam, and balsa wood. Except for the black rubber traction pad near the tail, the deck was covered with bold graphics in neon colors. The underside was glossy white and sported three curved, triangular fins at the tail. The board's leash — a long urethane rope with an ankle strap at one end — was attached to the tail.

When Kai reached his board, he secured the strap around his ankle. Then he picked up his board and headed back into the ocean. He floated the shortboard in front of him, pushing it along until the water reached his waist. With one smooth motion, he slid facedown onto the center of the deck. He pulled his arms through the water in even strokes, paddling away from shore.

Kai was as comfortable in the sea as he was in his own bed. He'd grown up playing in the sand and surf of this stretch of Southern California beach. Kai's father had once been a professional surfer, and he made sure that his son respected the awesome and unpredictable power of the sea. When Kai showed an interest in surfing, his dad had taught him the rules of safety before they even began with the basics of the sport.

That was four years earlier, when Kai was ten. Since then, he had become as confident on his shortboard as other fourteen-year-old boys were on skateboards and snowboards. He couldn't imagine a life without surfing — and hoped he'd never have to.

Kai continued to pull himself along through the water. He wasn't alone. Eleven other people were out surfing. Some sat on their boards, watching for a good wave. Others, like Kai, were paddling out to join the lineup — the place where surfers waited their turn to surf. Only two people were actually standing on their boards and slicing their way back toward shore.

Kai reached the lineup and sat up. As he bobbed on the waves, a cool breeze blew across his face, arms, and chest. He adjusted the neck of his long-sleeved rash guard shirt. He was glad he'd decided to wear the shirt instead of going bare chested. Not only did the stretchy fabric keep his chest from being scraped by the board, it kept him warm!

Kai looked out to sea and spotted a decent swell. He glanced around. No one else was making a move to take it so he decided to go for it.

He lay down on his board and stroked

hard to stay ahead of the wave. Then he felt it — the moment the wave surged beneath him and started pushing him forward. *Now!* instinct told him.

In one explosive move, he shot from a prone to a standing position. His stance was practiced and sure: feet shoulder width apart, left foot forward, right foot planted on the traction pad, and knees bent. He stretched his arms out and leaned forward for balance.

He'd caught the peak of the wave perfectly. It was a "left," a wave that broke from his left side toward his right. He rode the swell frontside, with the white water boiling at his back and the crest rounding in front of him. The water beneath the board was like a living thing, rippling and strong. He pumped the board, pushing it up and down with his feet, hoping to get enough speed to reverse direction and catch some air. When he didn't, he rode the wave straight into shore instead.

Kai bailed when the water was a few feet deep. He pulled on the leash to bring the board back then returned to the lineup.

When he got there, Kai saw Vaughn, a boy he knew from school. Vaughn was with another boy who looked older and wore tinted swim goggles. The other boy looked vaguely familiar, but with those goggles, Kai couldn't place him.

"Hey, Vaughn, how're you doing?" he called, raising a hand in greeting.

Vaughn returned the wave. Kai paddled closer to them.

"What's up, Kai?" Vaughn said.

"Hopefully me on my board — and soon!" Kai replied with a grin.

Vaughn laughed. "Yeah, I'm hoping to get in a few good runs, too." He introduced the other boy. "Kai, this is my cousin, Roger. He's visiting for the weekend."

Roger nodded then turned back toward where the waves were forming. Kai studied the boy's profile, more certain than ever that he'd seen Roger somewhere before. He decided to satisfy his curiosity.

"You look kind of familiar," he said to Roger. "You ever surf here before?"

"No," Roger muttered.

"Roger usually rides farther up the coast," Vaughn added hurriedly.

"Oh yeah?" Kai said with interest. "I've surfed some places up there, too. I bet that's where I saw you."

"Doubt it," Roger said. "I surf at a private beach."

Kai looked excited. "But I still could have seen you there! My dad took me to a private beach up the coast last year. The waves were killer!" He smiled ruefully.

"Unfortunately, the rocks under the waves were killer, too. I rolled over one that cut my leg something fierce. See?" He pointed to a three-inch-long, jagged, white scar on his left thigh. "I almost passed out when I saw the blood."

Vaughn made a face. "Gross. Don't tell me you kept surfing!"

"I wanted to, but my dad made me go to the first aid station. By the time I got it fixed up, we had to leave," Kai said.

"How come?" Vaughn asked curiously.

"The beach was being closed down so some movie company could shoot a surfing scene that afternoon." Kai rolled his eyes. "Someone told me the star of the movie was afraid he'd be mobbed by fans. Talk about ego, huh?"

Kai expected Vaughn to agree with him about how silly movie stars could be. Instead, Vaughn glanced at his cousin then dropped his gaze to the water.

Roger lifted his goggles and fixed Kai with a cold stare. "What do you know about it?" the older boy said. "Maybe the guy just wanted a little privacy. I mean, I bet if you're an actor you get recognized all the time. I bet people won't leave you alone — even if that's all you want." He fit the goggles back in place, spun his board, and paddled furiously away to catch the next wave.

Kai stared after him open-mouthed. He'd finally realized where he'd seen Roger before.

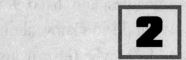

2

That's — that's — he's —" Kai sputtered.

"Shhh!" Vaughn hissed.

"He's the star of that movie!" Kai couldn't believe it. His eyes were glued to the figure surfing. Roger's board glided over the waves like a knife spreading peanut butter — smooth and effortless.

Kai's voice rose with excitement. "Look at him go! Wow! He looks just like he did in *Surfer Dude!*"

"Will you pipe down?" Vaughn begged.

Kai moved his board closer to Vaughn.

"Your cousin is R. William Masters, the actor?! You know I love his movies! Why didn't you ever tell me? And why didn't you call me and let me know he'd be surfing here today?"

Vaughn raised his hands in surrender. "I didn't tell you because Roger didn't want anyone to know he'd be here. He's sick of dealing with fans. He came here because people keep bugging him where he usually surfs. He just wants some peace and quiet."

Suddenly Kai remembered something. "I know why he's here!" he practically shouted. "He's looking for extras to be in his next movie, isn't he? I read in some magazine about how he does that! That's what he's doing, isn't it? Oh, man, do you think he'd pick me?"

Vaughn rolled his eyes. "After you made

fun of him by saying he had a big ego? Good luck!"

Kai grinned broadly. "Aha! So I was right! He *is* here to recruit surfers for a movie!" He turned his board. "Well, I'm going to show him my stuff! Then I'm going to ask for a part in the movie."

Vaughn caught hold of Kai's leash. "Kai, wait! You've got it all wrong! Roger isn't here to look for extras. He just wants to get in some surfing — *without* being recognized!"

Kai looked at him in disbelief. "Without being recognized?" he echoed. "Oh, come on, Vaughn! The guy's in the *movies*. I bet he loves all the attention!" He gave a hard tug on his leash and pulled it free of Vaughn's grasp. "Listen, don't worry. I'll be discreet!"

He spun his board toward shore and signaled that he was going to take the approaching wave. He paddled hard, but he was so busy thinking about Roger that he mistimed his takeoff. Instead of catching the wave's sweet spot, he was bowled over by the curl. His board shot out behind him, and he turned a somersault under the water. He surfaced as quickly as possible and pulled his surfboard beneath him.

Well, that *was impressive,* he thought as he rode the next swell in to shore on his stomach. He looked around quickly to see if Roger had seen him get axed. The movie star was halfway out to sea again. Relieved, Kai lay down and began paddling back to the lineup for another ride.

On his way out he saw Vaughn taking a wave. He paused to watch him. Vaughn was riding goofy foot, with his right foot forward rather than his left. When the ride was over, he floundered to find his footing in the gentle undertow. Vaughn was an okay surfer, Kai decided, but nowhere near as good as his cousin. *Or me,* he thought.

Kai had drifted sideways while watching Vaughn. Now he paddled his board around until the nose was facing back out to sea. He met a big wave head on, duck-diving his board right through it.

When he reached the lineup, he searched for Roger. But Roger had already taken another wave in to shore.

Kai decided to wait for him to return. As he bobbed in the water, he thought about what he'd say to the actor. *I'll be totally cool, of course,* he told himself. *A fan, but not crazy like some over-the-top groupie.*

"Hey, kid, you gonna surf or you just gonna sit there like a duck on a pond?" An impatient surfer interrupted Kai's thoughts.

"I'm going to hang here for a bit longer," Kai shouted back.

"You could have said so sooner," the other surfer grumbled. He spun his board and took the next wave.

Meanwhile, Roger and Vaughn were rejoining the lineup. Kai called out to his idol.

"R. William, over here!" he yelled. His voice echoed over the waves. A few other surfers glanced their way. Vaughn shot him a warning look. Kai ignored it. "I am so stoked to meet you. I want you to know that I *totally* love your movies. *Surfer Dude* is my favorite."

"Kai, keep it down," Vaughn pleaded.

Kai continued as if Vaughn hadn't spoken. "So listen, sorry about that crack about you having a big ego. I didn't know you were R. William Masters, star of the silver screen, when I said it, you know? Honest mistake. So about your next movie —"

15

By now, more surfers were staring at the three boys. Suddenly, one of them pointed at Roger and gave a small cry of recognition. Then she began talking excitedly to the other surfers, gesturing at Roger the whole time.

Roger glared at Kai as if he were a disgusting bug he'd just found floating in his cereal bowl. "Thanks for nothing! I am so out of here!" He grabbed the next wave and blasted his way to shore.

Kai sat hunched on his board, open-mouthed with dismay. Meanwhile, the other surfers gave a shout and hurried to follow the movie star. Kai cringed when two of them nearly collided in their haste to catch up.

Kai turned to find Vaughn glaring at him with even more anger than his cousin had.

"Oops," Kai said.

"*Oops!?*" Vaughn exploded. "You completely ruined Roger's day, and that's all you can say? 'Oops'?"

Kai looked at the beach — and gulped.

Roger had made it to shore. But as he bent down to remove his leash, three surfers converged on him. Roger stumbled. He abandoned his board and started sprinting up the soft sand. Two of the surfers pursued him. Even at this distance, Kai could hear them shouting. They sounded like hound dogs baying after their quarry. The third surfer grabbed the abandoned board as if to steal it. But a hugely muscled man — Roger's bodyguard, Kai figured — stopped him.

Kai hung his head. "Oh, man, I am so sorry, Vaughn. I guess I messed up, huh?"

Vaughn snorted. "You *think*?" He gave Kai one last reproachful look then grabbed the next wave, riding it in to shore on his stomach.

17

Kai stared after him, his face hot with shame. "I guess this means I'm not getting into his next movie," he mumbled in a lame attempt to make himself laugh.

It didn't work.

3

Kai caught a few more waves, but his heart wasn't into surfing anymore. Finally, he gave up. That's when he noticed how low the sun was in the sky.

Oh man, he groaned inwardly. *If I don't hurry, I'll have to lug my board home by myself!*

Kai and his father had an arrangement. Mr. Ford worked a block away from the beach. On the days that Kai planned to surf, Mr. Ford brought Kai's board to work with him in his truck. Kai picked up the board on his way to the beach. When he was done surfing, he carried his board back to the truck and rode home with his dad. If Kai was more than ten minutes late, however, Mr. Ford assumed he'd gotten a ride with someone else. That wasn't always the case, unfortunately. Sometimes Kai just lost track of time.

Kai had once asked his father why he couldn't just drive the truck down to the beach and pick him up. His father had replied that he wasn't interested in chasing him down every afternoon. "You want a ride, you get yourself and your board here on time," he'd said.

With that in mind, Kai surfed directly into shore on the next wave. He hurried out of the water and up the beach, pausing a second to take off the leash and grab his towel and sandals. He stopped again in the hose-off area, where he splashed water all over his board and then turned the hose on himself. When he'd removed most of the salt from his body and his board, he draped his towel around his neck, tucked his board under his arm, and speedwalked the block to his father's truck.

He was too late. The parking spot where the truck had been earlier was empty.

"Drat!" Kai muttered. He leaned his board against a fence rail and glanced around, hoping to see someone he knew who might offer him a ride. But the few people he saw were unfamiliar. With a sigh, he hoisted the board under his arm again and began to trudge home.

This day just gets better and better, he thought sarcastically.

His usual route took him on a wooden boulevard with gift shops and fast food restaurants. His favorite place was a seafood joint called the Shark Attack. As he walked by it, the smell of fried fish made his mouth water. He wished he had his wallet with him, but it was in his backpack, which he had left in his father's truck when he'd picked up his board earlier.

He was wondering what his father was making for dinner, when his thoughts were interrupted by the sounds of rock music. He stopped and looked around. Then his eyes widened in surprise.

Two doors down from the Shark Attack was a shop that had been closed for months, its plate-glass windows soaped up so passersby couldn't see inside. Now, however, the windows were clear. Kai grinned for the first time in an hour when he saw what was inside.

Gleaming surfboards of various lengths and widths lined one window. In another, rash shirts, leashes, and wet suits dangled on hangers. Next to the door was a railing with a sign that read "Park Your Board

Here." Above the open doorway was a banner announcing the grand opening of the Seaside Surf Shop. The rock music Kai had heard was coming from the shop.

Like a moth drawn to a flame, Kai followed the music. He parked his board then stepped inside the shop. It took his eyes a moment to adjust to the dim light. When he could see better, his grin grew even wider.

"This," he said out loud, "is paradise."

"Glad you think so," came a voice from behind him. "I kind of like it here myself."

Kai spun around to see a woman emerge from the back of the store. She was carrying an armload of surf booties and smiling pleasantly. "Let me know if you need help with anything." She started stacking the booties onto a shelf.

"Uh, okay," Kai mumbled, embarrassed to have been caught talking to himself. He picked up a pair of neoprene gloves and started to tug one on.

The woman frowned. "Just remember, you break it, you buy it."

Startled, Kai pulled the glove off. He edged toward the door. "Sorry."

The woman broke into a hearty laugh. "I'm kidding. Except for those tacky snow globes over there," she said, nodding her head at a display near the cash register, "I don't think there's anything here that can break. Really. Look around all you want. Touch stuff all you want, too."

Kai relaxed and did as she suggested. He was no expert, but to his eye the store was stocked with quality equipment — except for the snow globes, which *were* pretty cheesy looking. He sneaked a peek at the woman. She was tall, tanned, blond, and athletic looking. Even stacking booties, her movements were graceful. She was strong,

24

too, Kai realized as he watched her move a tall wooden bookcase with ease. He concluded that she was a surfer or at least had been a surfer at one time. He decided to see if he was right.

"So, um, you do much surfing around here?" he asked.

"Nope. You?"

"Yeah, I ride the waves right out at the beach here." He picked up a snow globe and shook it. Fake snow floated down on a mermaid sitting on plastic coral. "So, where *do* you surf?"

The woman walked behind the counter. "What makes you think I'm a surfer?"

Kai raised his shoulders. "You just seem like one, that's all," he said.

She grinned. "You've got good instincts." She leaned on the counter. "I used to surf. Now I own a shop. What's your name?"

"Kai, Kai Ford," he said. He stuck out his

hand. As she shook it, Kai noticed a scar running up her arm.

"Hey, did you get that scar surfing?" he asked.

She withdrew her hand. "Yes," she answered.

"I've got a scar from surfing, too," Kai said. "I took a digger on a rock covered with barnacles. Is that how you got yours?"

"Mmmm," she mumbled.

Kai wasn't sure if that was a yes or no. He was about to ask her more but she changed the subject.

"So, your name is Kai, as in the Hawaiian word for 'the sea'?"

Kai nodded. "Now I know you're a surfer. Only someone who surfs — or speaks Hawaiian — would know something like that!"

"*Used* to surf, Kai. Used to surf." She ducked under the counter.

Curiosity tickled his brain. *Why*, he wondered, *didn't she surf anymore?* Looking around, it seemed obvious to him that she was still into the sport. And she certainly seemed physically fit. *Was it something to do with the scar?*

She straightened up and put a stack of papers on the counter. "Tell me, Kai, are you any good at surfing?"

Kai shrugged. "I'm not bad. Not the best, but not the worst."

"Can you do any tricks?"

"Some." He ticked off the maneuvers he could do on his fingers. "I'm pretty good at catching air, so I can do different grabs. You know, stalefish, indy, double, things like that. My floater reentry and snaps aren't bad, either."

The woman nodded appreciatively and handed him one of the papers. "I'm sponsoring a surf contest for kids this weekend.

The winner gets a gift certificate for any of the merchandise you see here." She made a grand sweeping gesture with her arm, like a game show hostess showing off a fabulous prize. "I thought you might like to enter." "And," she added, waggling her eyebrows mischievously, "I thought you might tell your surfer friends to visit the shop, too. To pick up an entry form, that is!"

Kai had been in a few surf contests before. He'd never won first prize, but he'd always enjoyed being part of the competition. He looked around the shop again. Maybe this time he'd get lucky and surf his way to a pair of neoprene gloves or a new leash or maybe even a second board!

He started to fold the paper when he realized he didn't have any place to put it. His backpack was at home by now and while his swim trunks had pockets, they were still damp. The paper would just get wet. And he already had to carry his board and his towel.

The woman seemed to understand his dilemma. "Hold out your arm and roll up your sleeve," she instructed. Mystified, Kai did. She pulled the top off a marker and wrote down a Web site address on his skin. "You can download the entry form from this site," she said. She put the cover back on the marker. Then she stopped and, staring at the marker, gave a cry of dismay.

"Oh no! Permanent marker!"

"What?!" Kai looked at his arm in horror, certain that he'd be stuck wearing the Web address forever.

"Made you look!" the woman said, laughing. "Don't worry. It'll come off with soap and water. Just be sure to write the address down before you wash up for dinner!"

"Dinner! Oh my gosh! My dad's going to kill me if I don't get home!" Kai said.

"Thanks for the info about the competition. Great store. See you again!" He hurried out the door, grabbed his board, and jogged the remaining blocks back to his house, sandals slapping on the pavement and towel bouncing around his shoulders.

4

Have a nice run?" Kai's father looked up from the grill, a smile on his lips. The smile widened when he saw the sweat rolling down his son's face. "Lost track of time again, huh?" he said.

Kai was so out of breath he could only nod.

"Why don't you hit the shower before dinner? I'll throw a burger on for you when I hear the water stop."

Kai nodded again then carried his board inside the mudroom and leaned it next to his father's longboard. He went into the bathroom and turned on the shower. Just as he was about to strip down, he remembered the Web site written on his arm. He padded back to his room and jotted the address on a scrap of paper. In the shower at last, he sudsed the writing and his sweat away.

The smell of dinner made him dress in a hurry. He had been hungry when he stopped at the surf shop. Now he was famished!

He pulled the condiments from the refrigerator and put them on the table just as his father came in from the deck with a plate of burgers. Kai grabbed the top one, slathering the meat with ketchup and mustard. He added a pickle slice, capped it with a bun, and took an enormous bite.

Mr. Ford followed his son's lead. "Anything interesting happen today?" he asked as he started eating.

Kai looked up. He'd nearly forgotten the problem he'd caused at the beach earlier. He wondered if his dad had heard about R. William being there. It was possible — after all, his father worked close to the beach.

But his father didn't seem to be asking about anything in particular. So Kai decided not to mention what had happened. Instead, he finished chewing and said, "Well, there's a new surf shop on the boulevard. It's got totally cool stuff. And the woman who owns it is holding a competition on Saturday. The winner gets a gift certificate to her store."

"Interesting," his father said. "Are you going to enter?"

"Probably," Kai replied. "She gave me

the Web site address where I can download an entry form. I bet the site shows stuff from her store, too. Want to take a look at it with me after dinner?"

"Sure. I could use some new supplies myself."

Although Mr. Ford had given up his career as a professional surfer more than a decade ago, he still loved riding the waves. Kai had grown up hearing tales about his father's "golden days of surfing," as he put it. The stories were set in exotic surf spots like Sunset Beach (in Hawaii), Kirra Point (in Australia), and Puerto Escondido (in Mexico). Kai hoped to visit those spots one day.

After dinner, Kai and his father tidied the kitchen then carried their desserts (big bowls filled with ice cream) into the office. Kai logged onto the Internet and typed in the address the woman had given him.

A moment later, the screen was filled with an image of the surf shop's front door. Kai clicked on the door. The sound of rushing water came out of the computer speakers as a simulated wave washed away the door to reveal the interior of the shop. A line of text invited him to click on any of the merchandise to see what brands the store carried. Kai and his father looked at a few things, then Kai moved the curser to a graphic labeled "Surf Contest." When he clicked on it, the shop interior dissolved into a copy of the entry form the woman had given him earlier.

Kai was about to click on PRINT when suddenly his father grabbed the mouse from him.

"Hey!" Kai cried, startled. "What gives, Dad?"

5

Mr. Ford didn't answer. He had moved the cursor to a line of text near the bottom of the page and was trying to click on it. But it was just text, nothing hidden within it.

"'Sunny Pierce,'" Mr. Ford read part of the text aloud. "I wonder . . ." He had a dreamy, faraway look in his eyes.

Kai waved a hand in front of his father's face. "Hello? Dad? Are you still in there?"

Mr. Ford seemed to shake himself back to the present. He turned to look at his son. "Say, Kai," he said, his voice sounding overly casual to Kai's ears, "what did this woman shop owner look like?"

Kai raised his eyebrows. "Like a surfer, I guess. Blond, muscular, probably around your age, I guess. Why? Do you know her?"

His father ran his fingers through his hair. "I might know *of* her. Hang on a second." He got up and left the room.

Mystified, Kai took control of the mouse again and clicked on the PRINT button. The printer was spitting out the entry form when his father came back. He was holding an old surfer magazine, one from a large collection he'd saved from his years on the professional circuit. He flipped it open and pointed to a picture.

"That's not the woman you saw today, is it?" His father's voice had an excited edge to it.

Kai examined the picture. It showed a

woman tubing deep inside the barrel of a magnificent blue green wave. Kai whistled with appreciation.

"Is it her?" his father prodded.

Kai looked closely. Unfortunately, the woman's face was partly obscured by her right arm. "I don't know, Dad," he said finally. "Maybe, maybe not. Why?"

The dreamy look came back to his father's face. "That's a picture of Sunny, one of the best female surfers of my day. I'm telling you, Kai, you look up the phrase 'poetry in motion' and you'll see a picture of her."

Kai regarded the photo with new interest. "If she was so great," he asked, "how come I've never heard of her?"

Mr. Ford frowned slightly. "There's a big mystery surrounding her, actually. Take her name, for instance. She only went by Sunny, no last name. And like I said, she was the best, tops in the sport — for a few months, anyway. Then one day — *Poof!* She vanished from the scene. Just dropped out completely."

"Why?"

His father shook his head. "That's the mystery. There was never any explanation. She just withdrew from every event she was entered in. As far as I know, Sunny never surfed competitively again."

"Wow. So you think that Sunny Pierce, the woman who owns the shop, is this same surfer woman?" Kai's eyes sparkled. "That would be so cool! Do you have any more photos of her? Maybe I could see her face better in a different shot."

But his father shook his head. "She was around for such a short time that there are hardly any pictures of her. This magazine was planning to do a big article on her, but she disappeared before they got the chance. That photo is the only one I know of."

Kai studied the photo some more. Then he saw something he'd missed before. Or rather, he *didn't* see something that *should* have been there.

The arm in the photo was tanned a deep brown. But it didn't have a scar. If Sunny the surfer and Sunny the shop owner were the same person, the arm in the photo should have had a scar, too.

Kai broke the news to his father as gently as he could. His father looked crushed.

"Oh well, I suppose it was long shot," he said, thumping the magazine against his leg. "The California surf scene is probably filled with people named Sunny, after all. Still . . ."

"Dad, did you have a thing for her or something?" Kai asked with a grin.

Mr. Ford reddened. "I'll admit that I loved watching Sunny surf. But I was in love with your mother at the time, Kai." He glanced at the magazine again. "I always hoped I'd get a chance to meet Sunny. Oh well." He left the room, muttering to himself.

Kai's eyes strayed to a photo of his mother hanging on the wall. His parents had been divorced for nearly twelve years. Sixteen years ago, they had both been professional surfers. Soon after Kai was born, however, his father — a mediocre surfer at best — decided he'd rather stay home with his son than continue traveling the world in pursuit of a surfing title he'd probably never win. Kai's mother, on the other hand, wanted to keep competing. In the end they realized it was better that they divorce. Kai's father got custody of their two-year-old son. His mother surfed for another four years before finally ending her career. By that time she'd met and married another man. Now she lived on the East Coast with a new family. Kai saw her a few times a year.

Many people assumed that since Kai had never lived with both parents, he didn't miss having a mother around. They were wrong. Kai loved his father, but sometimes he couldn't help feeling sad when he saw other boys with their moms.

Kai tore his eyes from his mother's picture and turned back to the computer. He was about to log off the Web when the computer screen went completely black.

"Oh no!" Kai groaned. He clicked the mouse a few times then hit the Ctrl+Alt+Delete buttons, hoping that the screen would miraculously spring back to life. It didn't.

"Dad!" Kai called wearily. "Call the computer guy. We crashed again."

6

The next day was Sunday, which meant two things. One, Kai could spend the whole day at the beach. And two, the broken computer would remain broken for one more day. Their computer guy didn't work on Sundays.

Since the computer wasn't working, Kai's father had to go into the office to finish some paperwork he'd planned to do at home. That was a happy circumstance for Kai because it meant his dad could bring his board in the truck. His father put his own longboard in as well.

"I'd like to get in some surfing today, too," he said as he searched for his car keys. "Want a lift to the beach?"

Normally, Kai would have jumped at the offer. But instead he volunteered to stay behind and pack up a lunch for them to share later. "And I want to drop off the entry form at the surf shop, too," he told his father.

"I'll see you around noon, then."

After his father left, Kai grabbed some juice from the refrigerator then retrieved the contest form from the office and sat down at the kitchen table to fill it out. The top half of the form outlined the details of the competition. Kai read this part carefully.

The rules stated that contestants would start out in groups of four. Each group would have fifteen minutes to surf up to ten waves. The judges would pick the top two surfers from each group. Those two would advance to the next round of competition. Eventually, the best two surfers would compete in a final round to decide the winner.

The judges would evaluate the contestants' surfing technique, the length of their rides, the difficulty of their maneuvers, and how well they executed those maneuvers. Kai knew from previous contests that a surfer's style often played a large part in how the judges ranked him. Style was one part energy, one part ability to make surfing seem effortless, and one part risk taking. The surfer who made a series of difficult moves look easy and exciting was the surfer who walked away with the prize.

Kai had been surfing for four years, but he was still working on his style. Unlike other things his father had taught him, style was something he had to develop on his own.

Kai remembered how difficult surfing had seemed at first. The first year had been basic training. Using his father's longboard, he'd learned about safety, how to read a wave, how to pop up on his board and stay up, and how to bail when the ride wasn't going right. His father had called him a "grom," surfer lingo for a little kid who surfed.

At the start of his second year, Kai got his own board. He tested out different lengths before deciding to go with his shortboard. Shortboards were lighter and maneuvered better than longboards. Better maneuvering meant tighter turns and, eventually, fancier tricks.

Kai had been anxious to start doing tricks

right away. But once again his father started with the basics. "There are three turn techniques you have to know before you can go into tricks," he told his son. "The first is the bottom turn, when you spin the board around at the bottom of a wave and surf it to the top. The top turn directs the board the other way, from the top of the wave to the bottom. And last is the cutback. With this one, you move side to side across the wave."

He explained that the turn techniques usually helped a surfer gain speed and set up tricks. "The faster your board is moving, the better chance you have of staying upright. When the board wallows in the water, so do you."

Kai had practiced the turns until he could do them without thinking. Finally, on his thirteenth birthday, his father started teaching him more difficult maneuvers. Now, at fourteen, Kai could launch off the lip of a wave for an indy grab air, with his back hand on the toeside rail. He could usually pull off a floater reentry that found him turning in midair to ride the lip. He could do different snaps, too, riding up the wave for a 180-degree turn.

Kai looked at the form again. He knew if he was going to place high in this contest, he needed to put together a series of his best maneuvers. *But first,* he said to himself as he picked up a pen, *I have to get it in gear and fill out this form!*

7

Twenty minutes later, the completed form in hand, Kai approached the Seaside Surf Shop. He looked forward to seeing Sunny Pierce again. *Maybe I'll tell her about Dad's hopes that she was the missing surfer he wanted to meet all those years ago!* he thought with a smile.

But when he reached the shop, he saw a sign stating its Sunday hours as noon to five. It was only ten o'clock. He wasn't about to wait around for two hours, so he slipped the form under the door, where he was sure Sunny Pierce would see it. That

49

done, he continued on to his dad's truck to retrieve his board.

Soon he was paddling out to the lineup. The ocean was producing sizable waves with good curls that morning. Kai rode the first wave straight in frontside to test the swell's speed and momentum and to get his footing. The next time he did a few cutback turns, arcing his board back and forth across the face of the wave. On his third ride, he was planning to try a stalefish grab air. But he shifted his weight too far back and wound up digging the rail.

When he surfaced he paddled quickly to get out of the other surfers' way. He hoped no one had seen his fall. He thought he was in the clear, then he heard a familiar laugh and turned to see his father stroking his way toward him.

"Jeepers, who taught you to surf?" Mr. Ford said, grinning.

Kai grinned back. "Some guy who thought he was good enough to be a pro at one time!" he shot back. "Come on, I'll race you to the lineup!"

Kai and his father surfed together for another hour. Then they took a lunch break. Afterward, Mr. Ford lay on his towel for a quick nap.

The food and exercise had made Kai drowsy, too, so he lay down on his back and closed his eyes. But he couldn't sleep. Lights danced behind his closed lids. The salt from the seawater made his skin itchy. He scratched absently at the scar on his thigh.

Sometimes the scar itched — but nothing at all like it had itched when the gash was first starting to heal. Then he'd wanted to claw the bandage away to get at the irritation, even though he knew that scratching the cut would irritate it even more.

After all, the skin beneath the bandage was still red and raw. Later, when the bandage came off, the cut hadn't itched as much. The skin had gradually turned pink and then, as more time passed, smooth and white.

Kai knew his scar was ugly, but he was secretly proud of it. It was his first — his only — surfing injury. He couldn't imagine his leg without it.

Kai flopped over onto his stomach and looked at his watch. It was past noon. That meant the Seaside Surf Shop was open. He wondered if Sunny had found his form.

The sun was warm on his back. Kai rested his head on his arms, closed his eyes again, and let his thoughts wander from the upcoming contest to the stories his father told about the competitions he'd been in. He pictured the photo his father had shown him of the surfer Sunny and wondered where it had been taken. Once again, he wished that the surfer Sunny and Sunny Pierce were the same person, for his father's sake. But the lack of a scar on the surfer's arm proved they weren't.

Then something occurred to Kai. He sat up abruptly, his mind whirling.

What if they were *the same person —* *and the photo had been taken* before *Sunny had gotten the scar?*

8

Kai was so excited by his theory that he almost woke his father up to tell him about it. But he hesitated, remembering how disappointed his father had been last night. Kai decided to prove his theory before he got his father's hopes up. But how to get proof?

The obvious answer was to ask Sunny Pierce herself. Then Kai recalled how quickly she'd changed the subject when he asked her about her scar. It was obvious she didn't like to talk about how she got it.

Maybe I should just drop the whole

thing, Kai thought. But he couldn't get his mind off it. The possibility that he'd solved one of surfing's great mysteries was just too exciting. Finally, he shook his head as he thought, *How can I just drop it? Every time I go near that shop I'll be wondering. No, I have to know!*

He pondered how he might go about getting information on the mysterious Sunny. He decided to start his investigation by looking her up on the Internet.

Then he remembered his computer was on the blink. The library was closed on Sundays so those computers were out of reach, too. And Kai didn't dare ask his father if he could use the terminal at his workplace. Disappointed, Kai realized he couldn't do any investigating that afternoon. He hoped the home computer would be fixed by the next day, but he knew that it was unlikely.

It wasn't until many hours later, when he was lying in bed that night, that he thought of one other place he could get access to a computer.

His school library had a number of terminals. However, there was one problem. The library computers were off limits to students unless they had written permission to do research on them. The rule had been put into place a year earlier, after a group of students had been caught playing computer games instead of doing their work.

Kai wouldn't have a permission slip, of course. If he got caught he'd get two afternoons of detention. *Well, I'll just have to be sure I don't get caught!* he said to himself. *But how?* He stared at the ceiling of his room and devised a plan. When he was satisfied it would work, he rolled over and went to sleep.

✿   ✿   ✿

The first hours of school the next day dragged on endlessly for Kai. Finally, it was lunchtime — and time for him to put his plan into action. He wolfed down his sandwich then asked one of the lunch room monitors for permission to use the bathroom. But instead of going to the lavatory, he tiptoed into the library computer room.

The lights in the room were off. Kai crossed to the terminal farthest from the door and switched on the monitor. The screen glowed bright blue in the darkened room. Kai glanced nervously over his shoulder, certain he'd see a librarian bearing down on him and demanding to see his permission slip. But he was alone.

Every student had a password that gave them access to the school's network and the Internet. Kai typed quickly and in a matter of moments had a long list of Web sites containing the words "Sunny" and "surfing." He clicked on the first one and began reading.

Ten minutes later, he sat back and rubbed his eyes. He'd gone through six articles about surfing. All mentioned a talented up-and-coming surfer named Sunny and how she'd dropped out of the sport without explanation. Kai had hoped to see pictures, but so far the articles had been text only. He checked his watch and saw that he had only five minutes left before he needed to get to his next class. He leaned forward and clicked on the seventh article.

At that moment, the computer room was flooded with light. Kai spun around in his chair and came face-to-face with the head librarian.

"Oh, uh, hi, Ms. Kerns," he mumbled. "I — I was just, um, just . . . leaving?"

9

Ms. Kerns folded her arms across her chest and looked down her nose at Kai. "Tell me, Mr. Ford, what is so important for you to do on the computer that you had to break my rules?"

Kai hung his head. He knew Ms. Kerns was a stickler for rules. But she also had a reputation for being fair. Kai decided to appeal to her good side.

"My own computer is busted or else I would have waited until I got home to do this research," he said, hoping the word "research" would soften her up a bit.

Ms. Kerns eyeballed the list of articles he'd pulled up. She drummed her fingers against her arm. She seemed to be considering something. Kai's hopes rose. Maybe he wouldn't be given two days of detention after all.

"I'll tell you what, Kai," she said finally. "Since this is your first offense, I'm willing to make a deal with you."

Kai suddenly felt apprehensive. *What kind of a deal would a librarian want to make? Would he have to read a whole stack of books? Or shelve a countless number of titles? Or worse yet, read a story aloud to a group of first graders?* He'd heard of other kids doing that — it sounded horrifying to him.

"As you may know, I am the advisor for the school magazine."

The school magazine was a twice-monthly publication put together by students. It featured articles on school and community activities, interviews with teachers, and a list of upcoming events. Kai hadn't known Ms. Kerns worked with the students on it, but he nodded as if he did.

"It just so happens we are short one article this issue," Ms. Kerns continued. "So here's the deal: you write a 1000-word piece on surfing for the magazine, to be delivered to my desk no later than Friday after school, and I'll overlook the fact that you broke into my computer room. Agreed?"

Kai gulped. Two days of detention suddenly didn't seem so bad! Then he remembered about the surf contest. He wanted to get in as much practice time as he could between now and the competition. Detention took place after school — prime surfing time. He couldn't afford to spend two afternoons sitting in study hall instead of riding the waves. On the other hand, he could research and write the article after supper, when he wasn't allowed to surf.

He realized Ms. Kerns was waiting for an answer. "Uh, is there anything particular about surfing you want me to write about?" he asked.

Ms. Kerns smiled. "Just so long as it is interesting, informative, and factual, not simply a story about what it feels like to surf, you may write what you wish." Just then a bell rang, signaling the end of lunch period. "Okay, Kai, off you go. I look forward to reading your work."

By the end of school that day, Kai was still trying to figure out what he'd write about. When he stepped outside, the sun was shining, there was a stiff breeze, and his surfboard and gear were ready and waiting in the back of his father's truck.

I'll just go surfing for a little while, he told himself as he veered toward the shore. *I'll work out the article when I get home.*

Kai loved going surfing right after school. Unlike the weekends, the ocean wasn't crowded with surfers and he could usually get in a good number of runs without having to wait too long.

When he hit the beach that afternoon, he was happy to see that only a few other people were riding the waves. He soon realized why, however. The surf was choppier than usual. That meant surfing was going to be more difficult. But Kai didn't care. He had a contest coming up. The more practice he got in, the better.

He changed quickly in the bathhouse and then grabbed his board and ran into the surf. He planned to work on a series of three moves to do for the upcoming competition. He'd start with a bottom turn, gaining speed as he hurtled up the wave. Then he'd launch into a double grab air off the lip. And finally, assuming he was still standing after grabbing the rails, he'd try a tailside reentry, coasting back down the wave looking over his shoulder.

He went over each move in his head as he paddled out to the lineup. He did a few easy runs to get the feel of the day's waves. After his third ride, he was ready to try the tricks. He dangled his legs in the surf, watching for his turn and working hard to keep his balance in the choppy water.

Just then, he heard someone call his name. He glanced around and saw Vaughn paddling toward him.

Kai felt a stab of uneasiness. He wondered if Vaughn was still mad about the other day. A close look at his friend's face told him he was.

"I've been looking for you," the other boy

said, his voice laced with anger. "You really goofed things up for my cousin on Saturday, you know! Not only did you mess up his surf time, but someone almost stole his board!"

Kai opened his mouth to apologize. Then suddenly he felt something nudge his foot. He looked down and saw a large shadowy shape swim beneath him. A moment later a triangular fin cut the surface of the water then disappeared beneath the waves. Before his brain could process what he was seeing, he heard Vaughn gasp a single word that turned his blood to ice.

"Shark!"

10

Kai pulled his legs out of the water as quickly as he could. Vaughn did the same. Heart pounding, Kai knelt on his board, clinging tightly as waves rocked him from side to side and threatened to dump him into the cold ocean. He searched the sea, but the shifting surface made it difficult to see into the depths below.

Then he saw it — a torpedo shape rising up toward him. He squeezed his eyes shut, waiting for dagger-like teeth to sink into his board and topple him helplessly into the surf.

Instead, he heard a loud puffing sound. A gentle mist that smelled faintly of fish wet his face. His eyes flew open and he found himself staring into a shiny, blue black eye. A moment later the eye — and the sleek body attached to it — disappeared beneath the waves.

Kai almost sobbed with relief. The creature wasn't a shark. Shark eyes were flat and dull, the eyes of a killer. The creature that had looked at him just now showed intelligence and good humor.

"It's not a shark, Vaughn!" he called excitedly. "It's a dolphin! A bottlenose dolphin!"

Kai had heard other surfers talk about sharing waves with dolphins. Dolphins didn't attack people; in fact, there were many accounts of dolphins helping humans who were being threatened by sharks. And according to eyewitnesses, the graceful mammals with the built-in smiles seemed to love playing in the surf as much as the humans.

Kai had always wanted to surf with a dolphin. He sat up on his board and scanned the water, hoping the mammal would surface near him again.

Vaughn hung around, too. His earlier anger seemed to have vanished in the wake of the scare. Kai seized on the change of mood and apologized to his friend again and again for causing problems for his cousin.

Vaughn finally started laughing. "Okay, enough!" Then he sighed. "I just feel bad for my cousin, you know? He loves to surf, but ever since he started making movies he can't catch a wave without people hounding him. I'd promised him he'd be left alone here. He trusted me, and I let him down."

Kai felt lower than a sand flea. He was about to apologize yet again when suddenly the dolphin broke though the water between their boards, heading in toward shore. Kai and Vaughn exchanged delighted looks.

"Come on!" Vaughn yelled. They spun their boards to follow the animal. The dolphin seemed to want their company, for instead of swimming away it lingered in the surf. And when a wave formed at their backs, the dolphin rode the white water with them before turning back out to sea.

"That was so cool!" Vaughn cried. "C'mon, let's see if we can find it again!"

Kai and Vaughn paddled back out to the lineup. Twice more the dolphin swam alongside them. Then it splashed farther out to sea where it joined a number of other dolphins. That was okay with Kai. He knew he'd remember catching the waves with the graceful animal for a long time.

He was glad Vaughn had been there to share the experience, too. It helped patch things up between them. Before their next ride, Kai told Vaughn about the surf shop and the contest.

"I know all about it," Vaughn told him. "Gonna win me a new board for my quiver!"

"Oh yeah?" Kai said with a smile. "You got to beat me first, pal! Check out these moves!"

For the next half hour, Kai practiced his three maneuvers. The less-experienced Vaughn worked on some simpler tricks. When it was time to leave, the two boys walked up the beach together.

"I gotta get going. See you at school, Kai," Vaughn said after he'd rinsed off.

Kai waved good-bye, finished cleaning his board, and hurried to his father's truck. He'd made it in time for a ride. On the way home, Kai told his father all about the dolphins. "Sure am glad they weren't sharks," he said, shivering a bit as he remembered his initial fright.

"You and me both!" his father said. "I've never witnessed a shark attack on a surfer. They don't happen that often, fortunately. Still, it's important to remember that when we're surfing, we're in their turf. You see one, you get out of the water as quickly — and quietly — as you can."

As Kai listened to his father, he suddenly had an inspiration for his magazine article. He would write about shark attacks on surfers — where they happened, why they

71

happened, and what surfers could do to prevent them from happening. He could open with a story of one such attack then follow up with the dos and don'ts of sharks and surfing. After that day's scare, he realized it was information he'd like to learn about too!

11

After dinner that night, Kai did his assigned homework. Then he asked his father if he had any books on sharks. When his father wanted to know why he needed such a book, Kai confessed about what had happened at the library. Mr. Ford chewed him out for a full five minutes, telling him how disappointed he was Kai had broken school rules. Then he pointed Kai toward the computer and told him to get working.

"But, Dad, isn't the computer broken?"

His father looked embarrassed. "Turns

out it was just a loose connection. I could have repaired it myself in a second instead of calling in the repair guy."

Kai groaned inwardly. *If only Dad had tried fixing the computer on Sunday, I wouldn't be stuck writing this article!* he thought.

But he *was* stuck, and he knew the sooner he started the work the sooner he'd be done. He logged onto the Internet, pulled up a number of sites containing the words "shark attack" and "surfing," and began reading.

He soon found himself engrossed in his subject. He learned that shark attacks on swimmers and surfers were rare, with an estimated fifty to seventy-five people attacked per year. In fact, people were more likely to be struck by lightning or killed by an elephant than fatally wounded by a shark.

Scientists classified three types of attack — encounters, provoked attacks, and unprovoked attacks. Encounters were chance meetings of humans and sharks. There was no contact between the two species during these meetings; they simply were in the same place at the same time. Provoked attacks, on the other hand, did involve contact. These attacks happened when a human did something the shark may have found threatening, like trying to touch it. Then the shark was likely to defend itself by biting the human. And finally, there was the unprovoked attack, when a shark went for a human for no apparent reason. Many researchers thought unprovoked attacks happened because the shark mistook the human for a seal, sea lion, or other kind of prey.

Kai thought about what the underside of a surfboard must look like to a hungry shark and realized it probably resembled a tasty meal. One article mentioned that some surfers painted large eyes on the bottom of their boards as a way of scaring off sharks. Remembering how frightened he'd been when he thought the dolphin was a shark, Kai decided to paint some eyes on his own board — and soon!

When it came to preventing an attack, people were advised to use common sense. One rule of thumb was not to swim or surf alone or where sharks were known to swim. People were also advised to keep an eye on other sea creatures swimming near them too. If those creatures started acting differently — if seals suddenly left the water, for instance — the swimmers should follow suit because it could mean a shark was nearby. Shiny jewelry or flashy clothing might look like the scales of a fish to a shark, so swimmers were told not to wear such things. They were also advised not to thrash around when in the water; such violent motions mimicked those of an injured seal or other shark prey. And finally, it was recommended that surfers and swimmers stay away from places where people are fishing — sharks are attracted to motion and the scent of blood.

Kai's hand strayed to his scar when he read that last piece of advice. He wondered if his father had ordered him from the water the day he was cut because he was afraid a shark would smell Kai's blood. The thought made Kai shiver.

The next site he pulled up contained first-person accounts of attacks. Kai swallowed hard when he read about surfers who had been bumped off their boards by six-, seven-, and eight-foot sharks. The site had pictures of boards bitten nearly in two; one showed a razor-sharp shark tooth still embedded near the board's tail fins.

That site led him to another, written by a surfer named Raymond Phelps. Raymond had been the victim of a shark attack more than fifteen years ago. The site opened with a disturbing photo of the surfer actually being attacked. The photo was grainy, taken by an amateur photographer standing on shore. Even so, it was painfully clear what was happening in it. Raymond's arms and head were visible above the water — as was the tail of a large shark. The water surrounding the figures was a sickening mixture of white spray and red blood. Amazingly, Raymond had survived the attack, thanks in large part to a woman who had been surfing nearby.

That's when Kai saw that there was, in fact, a second surfer in the photo. The image of the attack was so arresting that Kai hadn't noticed her before. When he did, he sat bolt upright. The female surfer's right arm was wrapped in a bloody bandage, but that's not what had startled him. Even though the poor photo quality made it hard to see her face clearly, Kai was positive the surfer was Sunny Pierce.

12

Kai searched the article, praying Raymond had named the female surfer at some point. He found what he was looking for at the end. Raymond hadn't known the woman who had helped him; in fact, it was only when he was recovering in the hospital that he learned she was a talented surfer known only as Sunny. After helping him to shore, she had vanished. Despite many years spent trying to find her, Raymond had never been able to locate her.

A line at the bottom of the Web page

noted that the article had been posted within the past year. It also gave an e-mail address where Raymond could be reached if anyone wanted to comment on his story.

Kai felt a surge of excitement. With one simple e-mail message, he could reunite Raymond and his rescuer, thus putting an end to Raymond's fifteen-year search! Not only that, he'd learned that Sunny Pierce and Sunny the shop owner were, in fact, the same person.

Kai fished around in the desk drawer until he found the scrap of paper with the Seaside Surf Shop's Web site address. He copied down Raymond's e-mail address then called up his own e-mail account. He typed Raymond's address into the recipient box. In the message box he wrote, "Hi, you don't know me, but I know the woman who rescued you from the shark. To find her, check out this Web site!" He typed in the shop's address then hit "send" and logged off again.

And now, he thought gleefully, *to tell Dad that Sunny is working a few blocks from where his office is!* He shoved his chair back and hurried from the room in search of his father.

Mr. Ford was stunned when Kai told him of his discovery. He made Kai show him the Web site with Sunny's picture. He asked Kai repeatedly if he was "absolutely, positively certain" the woman in the picture was the same one who owned the shop.

"It's her, Dad," Kai answered again and again. "See that bandage on her arm? I bet the scar I saw was from that cut. It looks like she got hurt that day." He grinned broadly. "Man, I can't wait to talk to her about it! She sure will be surprised when she finds out we know who she is!"

Kai expected his father to join in his delight. Instead, Mr. Ford was silent. He frowned slightly, as if deep in thought. Then he shook his head.

"Kai, I'm not sure it's such a good idea for you to tell Sunny what you found out."

Kai's eyes bugged. "What? Are you kidding me? Of course I'm going to tell her! I'm going to tell everyone I know! I'm going to write about it for the school magazine, too!"

Mr. Ford caught his son by the arm. "Kai, stop and think for a minute!" He dropped Kai's arm and started pacing. "Sunny Pierce has kept her past secret for a long time. Don't you think if she wanted people to know, she'd tell them herself? After all, her background as a world-class surfer would certainly help bring customers into her store." He puffed air out of his cheeks. "Besides, we don't know the *whole* story, do we?"

"What do you mean?" Kai asked.

"We don't know why she stopped surfing, Kai. And frankly, I'm convinced it's none of our business."

"But —"

"No buts, Kai. Don't stick your nose in where it doesn't belong."

"What about my article for the magazine?" Kai wanted to know.

"You can write about shark attacks without mentioning Sunny, can't you?"

Kai nodded glumly.

"Okay, then," his father said, his voice no longer as stern. "That's that. I'll let you get to it."

Kai sat back down at the computer and stared at the article on the screen. He was about to close it when his gaze happened upon the e-mail address at the bottom of the page.

Uh-oh, he thought as he remembered the e-mail he'd sent. *I guess telling Raymond where to find Sunny wasn't such a good idea after all.*

13

Kai slept poorly that night, plagued by nightmares. In one, Roger was chasing him through the ocean, surfing on the back of an enormous shark that had jaws filled with daggers. "You ruined my day, now I'm going to ruin yours!" the actor yelled as the shark snapped at Kai's legs. Another dream found him floundering in knee-deep water behind Sunny Pierce, who kept begging him to leave her in peace.

He awoke the next morning with a pounding headache. The pain had subsided by the time he got to school, luckily.

He was walking down the hallway to his locker when he heard someone call his name. He turned to see Vaughn hurrying toward him.

"Hey, Kai," the other boy said in a low voice. "Listen, I thought I better warn you about something. You know that surf competition we're in this weekend? Well, guess who was asked to be one of the judges?"

Kai gave him a blank stare.

Vaughn looked around then leaned in closer. "My cousin, that's who!" he whispered hoarsely. "Seems he ducked into the surf shop when he ran from the beach that day. The owner let him hide in her back room until the crazy fans went away. In exchange for her help, Roger volunteered to be a judge."

Kai groaned. "Oh, great. I guess I can kiss any chance of taking home a prize good-bye," he mumbled.

Vaughn gave him a long look. "Well, you know you only have yourself to blame."

Kai blinked. "What do you mean?"

"Kai, I like you, but you have a bad habit of invading people's privacy sometimes. I mean, if you hadn't been so bent on figuring out who Roger was that day, you wouldn't be worrying about him now, would you?"

The bell rang. Vaughn headed off for his first class, leaving Kai to stare after him.

Two people in the past twenty-four hours had told him he was nosy. The realization that they might be right brought his headache back full force.

The rest of the week passed in a dull blur for Kai. He sat through classes, did his homework, and worked on his article. He went surfing a few times too, but he didn't bother to practice his tricks. After what Vaughn had told him about Roger being a judge, he had all but decided to pull out of the competition.

He checked his e-mail every night too, wondering if the message he'd sent had made it to Raymond. It hadn't been returned to him as undeliverable, so he guessed that it had. Then Thursday night he got an answer.

To the person who sent me the surf shop address, thank you! I haven't reached Sunny yet, unfortunately, but I plan to show up at the competition she's running. Perhaps I'll see you there, too.

Kai closed down his e-mail and put his head on the keyboard. *Terrific,* he thought.

On Friday, he delivered his magazine article to Ms. Kerns. She asked him to stay while she read through it. When she was done, she laid the paper on the desk and fixed him with a thoughtful look.

"This is quite good, Kai," she said finally. "Informative and interesting."

"Really? Uh, thanks," Kai said.

"In fact," she went on, "I think you would make a fine addition to our magazine staff. I know surfing is very popular with a lot of our students. What would you think about writing a regular column on the local surf scene?"

Kai looked at her in surprise. "Me? Be a writer?" he said. "I don't know." He thought back to the time he had put in researching and writing the article. He realized that even though he had dreaded the assignment at first, once he'd gotten into it, he'd kind of liked doing it. "I guess I could try," he said slowly.

Ms. Kerns smiled. "Excellent. As it turns out, I already have your next assignment."

She handed him a piece of paper. Kai nearly choked when he saw he was holding an announcement for the surfing competition.

"This contest is taking place on the beach tomorrow," she said. "I'd like you to cover it for our next issue."

Kai knew he couldn't refuse. How could he, when he'd just said he'd do it? Besides, she'd probably want to know why he wouldn't take the assignment; even though he had his reasons, he didn't think she'd appreciate them. In fact, she'd probably advise him to deal with the situation head on — grown-ups were like that. So instead, he folded up the paper and stuck it in his backpack.

"I'll be there," he promised.

14

The next morning, Kai woke up with a knot in the pit of his stomach. The surf competition was scheduled to take place later in the morning. He spent the time before it wondering whether he should simply drop out, observe the contest from the shore, and write the article based on what he'd seen. But if he did that, he'd have to explain to his father why he was dropping out. Plus, if he did stay on land, he stood a good chance of witnessing something he wasn't sure he wanted to see anymore, namely, the reunion of Sunny and Raymond. And what if Roger spotted him lurking in the dunes? For all he knew, the actor was still mad at him, maybe angry enough to have one of his bodyguards throw him off the beach!

What a stupid mess, he thought miserably. *And it's all my own fault. Vaughn's right. If I'd just minded my own business, R. William wouldn't have been run off the beach. Who knows what kind of grief my e-mail could cause Sunny and Raymond?*

Kai felt like a heel. If he could have turned back the clock, he would have. But he couldn't, and in the end he decided that if he had to be at the contest he might as well surf. So by mid morning he loaded his board into his father's truck and together they headed for the beach.

A large section of the beach was roped off. Signs around the area announced the competition as well as the presence of R. William Masters, movie star. Spectators were invited to stay and watch but were asked to steer clear of the surf until the contest was through.

Mr. Ford set up beach chairs and an umbrella while Kai joined the check-in line. The line was moving slowly, giving Kai time to scan the beach.

A decent-sized crowd had gathered. Still, Kai picked out Roger right away — the movie star would have been hard to miss, surrounded as he was by fans clambering for his autograph. Kai could hear the actor talking loudly and laughing.

Guess he's okay getting attention today, Kai thought.

He spotted Vaughn next. His friend waved then jerked a thumb at his cousin and shrugged as if to say, "Go figure!"

Kai continued to search the other faces on the beach. Although he'd never actually seen Raymond — the water in the photo had obscured his face — he thought he might be able to guess who he was by his age or his eagerness to find Sunny. But he didn't see anyone who fit that description.

Suddenly, Kai found himself at the front of the line — and face-to-face with Sunny. She smiled warmly at him.

"You're Kai, right?" she said.

He nodded.

"Okay, you'll be in the second heat. That's in about forty-five minutes. Go ahead in now and take some practice runs to get a feel for the day's surf, if you like, but come on out when you hear the horn. And good luck!"

Kai thanked her then retrieved his board

and swam out into the surf with the other competitors. The waves were fantastic and large with long, rolling curls. Kai wanted to kick himself for not working on his tricks the past week. But he hadn't, and now he had no one but himself to blame if he stunk up the water with poor surfing.

Ten minutes later he heard a long horn blast. He left the water with the other surfers and walked up the soft sand to where his father sat. Mr. Ford waved him into an empty chair and handed him a pair of binoculars.

"For checking out your competition," he said, lifting his own set up to his eyes.

The contest started five minutes later. Four surfers bobbed in the lineup. The horn sounded. In a flash, all four paddled like mad for the first wave. According to the contest rules, the first one up won possession of the wave. In this case, that honor went to a small girl in a bright green and black wet suit. She guided her board back and forth across the wave — *nothing fancy, but controlled and smooth,* Kai thought.

He was about to make a comment about the girl when he realized his father wasn't looking at her. Or at the ocean, for that matter. Instead, Mr. Ford's binoculars were trained on someone on land. Kai didn't bother turning his head. He knew who his father was looking at.

"Dad," he said. "Why don't you just go over to Sunny and introduce yourself?"

"I would," his father muttered, "but some other guy is about to beat me to her."

Kai quickly turned his own binoculars to that part of the beach. Sure enough, a muscular man was making his way across the sand to where Sunny sat. The man walked with a pronounced limp. Kai focused on the man's bare leg. He wasn't positive, but he thought he saw a jagged scar in the shape of a crescent — or the jaws of a shark — on the man's calf.

It's Raymond! he thought. *It has to be!*

Kai wanted to look away, but he just couldn't seem to put the binoculars down. From where he sat he couldn't hear their voices, but their gestures and expressions spoke volumes. It was like watching a silent movie.

First Raymond tapped Sunny lightly on the shoulder. Sunny turned — and stood up so quickly that she knocked her chair over. Her hand flew to her neck, and she seemed to be struggling for words.

Raymond appeared to be reassuring her. He picked up her chair, took her arm, and guided her back down to her seat. Sunny bent forward, head in hands, her long blond hair covering her face. Raymond crouched down next to her and continued to talk. At one point, Sunny looked up and shook her head violently. She pointed to the scar on her arm. Her face was laced with misery. Raymond talked some more, his movements calm and gentle. Finally, Sunny's expression softened. Raymond smiled and to Kai's great relief, Sunny smiled back. They stood and embraced.

"I wonder what *that* was all about!"

The sound of his father's puzzled voice broke the spell. Kai lowered his binoculars. He was about to tell his father all he knew when suddenly the horn blasted again. The first heat had ended.

"Hey, you're up!" Kai's father said. "Better get going or you'll miss your chance!"

Kai hesitated a moment then picked up his board and rushed into the surf. He promised himself he'd explain everything to his father later. Right now he had to put all his attention on surfing!

15

The water closed around Kai's head as he duck-dove his board through a wave. He reached the lineup at the same time as the three other surfers. Together, they bobbed on the surf, waiting for the signal to start their heat.

The horn sounded a minute later. Kai and the others paddled furiously, each hoping to be the first to catch the wave rising behind them. Kai thought he had it but then realized a bigger boy had beaten him to it. He sank back into the water and returned to the lineup to await the next swell.

When it came, he was ready. He stroked his way to the top. Another surfer got there at the same time. But Kai was closer to the lip's curl. According to the rules, that gave him possession of the wave. The other surfer was forced to drop out.

Each heat was fifteen minutes long. Kai figured he could catch at least five and maybe as many as seven waves in that time. He had to make the best of each one. So he decided to try his series of tricks right away. If he messed up, well, he'd still have other rides to try again.

He pumped the board to gain speed. Then he shifted his weight to make the board turn back toward the wave. He rode straight up the face and flew over the lip. When he was in the air he grabbed his rails with both hands at the same time. Then he straightened and landed right on the lip with the tail of his board facing shore. Moments later he'd ridden from the lip to the trough of the wave and was cutting back and forth through the white water into shore.

I did it! he said to himself, amazed with his own performance. *I really did it!* Adrenaline coursed through his veins. He spun his board around and flew back to the lineup for a second run.

Unfortunately, his next ride was a disaster. First off, he chose a poor wave, one that turned to mush soon after he popped up. Then as he was trying to get up speed, the surfer before him suddenly appeared directly in his path. Kai had to bail in order to avoid hitting him. When he surfaced he saw a third surfer beginning a run. He realized that if he didn't move quickly, he'd be in that surfer's way!

He swam frantically to the side and managed to give the surfer a clear path. He sighed with relief, knowing that if he'd caused her a problem he'd have lost precious points for interfering with her ride.

Kai caught three more waves in that heat, but none of his rides were as good as his first. *Still,* he thought, *that first one was strong enough to move me to the next round.*

Unless, of course, Roger decides to vote me out, he thought as he left the water.

Kai pushed the unwanted thought from his brain. After all, he wasn't even sure if Roger knew he was there.

Kai was on his way back to his chair when he noticed that his father wasn't there anymore. He looked around for him, then stopped in his tracks.

Mr. Ford was talking with Sunny — and Raymond!

Kai turned away quickly, hoping none of them had seen him. No such luck.

"Kai! Come over here right now!" his father bellowed.

16

His father fixed him with a steely glare. "Raymond here tells me he got a very unusual e-mail message earlier this week. The return address is ours. I'm quite sure *I* didn't send it." He folded his arms across his chest. "Well?"

Kai stared at his feet. "I was the one who sent it."

His father sighed loudly. "Oh, Kai, when are you going to learn to mind your own business?"

Kai dug his toes in the sand. "I'm very

sorry, Ms. Pierce, if I've caused you any problems because of it," he whispered. "I guess I kind of invaded your privacy. I'm sorry."

No one said anything for a moment. Then Sunny laid a gentle hand on his shoulder. Kai looked up, surprised to see her giving him a warm smile. "Thank you for your apology, Kai." She glanced at Raymond. "I'll admit I was shocked when I saw Raymond. After all, I'd spent many years trying to make sure he couldn't find me."

"Really? Why?" Kai blurted. Then he caught himself. "Uh, I'm sorry. You don't have to tell me. It's none of my business."

Sunny gave a small shrug. "It's okay. I don't mind telling you." She held out her arm and pointed to her scar. "You were right about this being from a surfing accident. I got it the day Raymond was attacked."

She dropped her arm and sat in her chair. "I was surfing off the coast of Australia. I had read stories about shark sightings in that particular spot earlier in the week, but because other people were surfing there that day, I figured the stories were exaggerated." She looked at Raymond again. "Obviously, I was wrong."

"Anyway, that surf spot was well known for its fantastic barrels. As you probably know, good barrels are often made near coral reefs. Well, long story short, I took a digger on a particularly sharp piece of coral. My arm was bleeding pretty badly, but I didn't get out right away because I wanted to practice tubing. When the bleeding didn't stop, I finally got out and wrapped it in a spare shirt." Her voice dropped to a whisper. "I didn't get out soon enough, though. My blood attracted a shark — the shark that attacked Raymond."

Raymond spoke for the first time. He had an Australian accent, Kai realized. "You have no way of knowing if that's true or not!"

He turned to Kai. "The water was pretty murky that day, as I recall. I was still learning to surf and found paddling out past the reef pretty tough going."

"You were wearing a black wet suit, weren't you?" Kai put in, remembering the photo.

Raymond nodded. "Exactly. So there I was, all in black and floundering around on my board in the murk. From a shark's point of view, I probably looked like a sick fish or something." He lifted his shoulders. "Easy prey."

"But the blood —" Sunny started to say.

"— may or may not have been a factor," Raymond concluded. "We have no way of knowing, Sunny! But I do know this. If you hadn't been there to help me that day, I'd be walking with a fake leg instead of just a limp. And," he added with a broad smile, "I would never have met my wife. She was my doctor, you see. We fell in love, got married, moved to the States, and have been living happily ever after since."

Kai's father suddenly perked up. "Oh, so you're married? That's nice." He looked at Sunny with new hope.

Sunny didn't seem to notice. "I've always blamed myself for your attack," she said. "If my blood hadn't been in the water, maybe it wouldn't have happened."

"Is that why you gave up surfing?" Kai asked curiously.

She nodded. "Every time I looked at my arm, I saw that shark grabbing hold of Raymond's leg. I felt so guilty I couldn't get on my board again."

Raymond looked horrified. "But that's

terrible! You were one of the best surfers on the scene! I never would have let you quit if I had known!"

Sunny smiled ruefully. "Guess I should have come to see you instead of running away." She sighed and gazed around at the ongoing surf contest. "Then again, as you can see, I didn't give up the sport entirely. And who knows? Maybe some day I'll ride again."

"You know," Mr. Ford said slowly, "I've got my longboard here. If you wanted to use it today, I'd be honored to lend it to you."

Sunny smiled. "I just may take you up on that, Alex," she said. "But now, I have to finish running this contest. Kai, would you do me a favor and ask the judges for the names of the winners of the last two heats?"

"Uh, sure," Kai said. He started to leave.

"Hold on, Kai." His father's stern voice called him back. "I hope you've learned a lesson here today. Just because things turned out right with Sunny and Raymond doesn't mean it's okay to butt your nose into other people's business. What you did could have caused them a lot of pain."

Kai hung his head. "I know, Dad." He looked from Sunny to Raymond to his father. "From now on I'll think before I act."

"Okay then," his father said. "Now go on and get that list."

Kai hurried across the sand toward the raised platform where the judges sat. His eyes fell on Roger — another victim of his thoughtlessness, he realized with a sharp stab of guilt. Well, he knew he couldn't leave things with Roger as they were now. He climbed the platform and tapped Roger on the shoulder.

"Excuse me, R. William?"

Roger regarded him through narrowed eyes. "What do *you* want?"

Kai gulped. "I want to say I'm very, very sorry for what happened the other day. I was totally out of line when I gave away who you were. I promise if you come surfing there again, I'll stay out of the water."

Roger blinked. Then he smiled. "That's okay, Kai. I wasn't happy with what you did, but I guess I've got to accept the fact that people are going to recognize me. Chances are, if you hadn't that day, someone else would have. And Kai? Don't clear the waves because of me. You're a good surfer. I wouldn't mind sharing the sea with you sometime." He handed Kai a piece of paper. "You better get this list of names to Sunny, pronto. You're in the next heat."

Kai glanced down and saw that he had indeed moved up to the next round. "Thanks, Roger!"

"See you in the surf, Kai."

Kai grinned. "It's my favorite place to be!" He started to leave, then stopped. "By the way, Roger, could I maybe interview you for my school magazine?" He put a hand over his heart. "I promise you I'll only write about what you want to tell me — no snooping!"

The #1 Sports Series for Kids

MATT CHRISTOPHER®

Read them all!

*Previously published as Crackerjack Halfback

All available in paperback from Little, Brown and Company

**Previously published as Pressure Play

Matt Christopher®

Muhammad Ali	*Mario Lemieux*
Lance Armstrong	*Tara Lipinski*
Kobe Bryant	*Mark McGwire*
Jennifer Capriati	*Yao Ming*
Jeff Gordon	*Shaquille O'Neal*
Ken Griffey Jr.	*Jackie Robinson*
Mia Hamm	*Alex Rodriguez*
Tony Hawk	*Babe Ruth*
Ichiro	*Curt Schilling*
Derek Jeter	*Sammy Sosa*
Randy Johnson	*Venus and Serena Williams*
Michael Jordan	*Tiger Woods*